<u>The Find of a Thousand Lifetimes</u>

The Story of the Gorto Site Discovery

by
James Robert Paquette

Enjoy this journey into the past.

James R Paquette

First published by AuthorHouse 07/18/05

ISBN: 1-4208-5431-3 (sc)

Library of Congress Control Number: 2005905376

Printed in the United States of America
Bloomington, Indiana

This book is printed on acid-free paper.

authorHOUSE

1663 LIBERTY DRIVE
BLOOMINGTON, INDIANA 47403
(800) 839-8640
www.authorhouse.com

This book is dedicated to the wonderful memory of "my little brother"
Ray Paquette (January 20, 1956—December 4, 2004).

On a cold December afternoon, it was Ray's turn to take to the timeless path of the
Paleo-Indians. All of us will someday set foot upon that same sacred path.
It seems so fitting that my brother was laid to rest upon a quiet terrace that overlooks
the east bank of the Carp River less than a mile from the Deer Lake Gorto Site.
We sent him on his way with a bundle of our finest hunting arrows and an ancient
quartzite knife. I also gave him that very first arrowhead that we found so many years
ago at Peminee Falls on the banks of the great Menominee River.
He was with me that summer day…and he is with me today.

Happy hunting, Ray-Ray!

. . . .

ACKNOWLEDGMENTS

I want to begin by thanking those who deserve it the most—my family. I will forever be grateful to them for understanding my passion to uncover ancient secrets and to relentlessly seek the treasures of the past. Without the undying support (better known as love) through the years of my wife Karen, my parents Pat and Bob Paquette, and "daddy's girls" Nicole, Jill, Jodi, and Kerrie, there would certainly be no book because there would be no great discoveries for me to write about. That I do know.

I want to thank John Gorto for being my friend and for allowing me to join him on that historic search for ancient sites on Deer Lake back in 1986-87.

I want to give special thanks to Dr. Marla Buckmaster for helping me live my childhood dream of someday being called an "archaeologist." Without her help, and most of all, her acceptance of my sometimes non-traditional approach to that science, my dream would still be just a dream.

I want to thank Cleveland-Cliffs Inc for allowing us to excavate at the Gorto Site back in 1987, and for donating that incredible collection of Deer Lake Late-Paleo-Indian artifacts to the people of the State of Michigan. I also want to thank Cliffs for their continued support of Marquette County archaeology as they graciously agreed to sponsor the publication of this very book.

I will end by thanking my Grandfather Medolph Paquette. He was a great human being who always spoke with pride of his French-Canadian and Native American ancestry, and in the process, ignited a burning passion in a little boy's heart to learn all that he could about the mysterious and unknown parts of his own heritage. It's a fire that will burn in my heart until the day that I also take to the sacred path of the Paleo-Indians.

Thank you, Grandpa! And, oh yah, Happy Hunting with Ray!

****

Lake Superior

Deer Lake
Gorto Site

Michigan

North

INTRODUCTION

This book accurately documents the 1987 discovery and subsequent excavation of one of the most remarkable archaeological sites ever uncovered in the Upper Great Lakes region. It was in the early spring of that year that avocational archaeologists John Gorto and I, quite literally, stepped upon a large treasure trove of ancient Late Paleo-Indian/Early Archaic period projectile points while conducting an archaeological survey in the drained basin bed of Deer Lake near Ishpeming, Michigan. Registered with the Michigan History Division as the Gorto Site (20MQ39), this Scottsbluff/Great Lakes Cody site (ca. 9500 to 8800 Radiocarbon Years Before Present or 10,800 to 9800 Actual Calendar Years Before Present) provided the absolute proof that I had been seeking to confirm my belief that truly ancient Native American peoples had once inhabited the central Upper Peninsula of Michigan as far back as perhaps the end of the last Ice Age.

The Gorto Site discovery and excavation received a good deal of local publicity back at the time, with minor amounts of regional news coverage. After the excavation, Dr. Marla Buckmaster/Northern Michigan University and I co-authored the necessary follow-up research report, "**The Gorto Site: Preliminary Report on a Late-Paleo Indian Site in Marquette County, Michigan.**" Since the publication of that report in **THE WISCONSIN ARCHAEOLOGIST (Vo.69. No. 3)** back in the late 1980's, this particular U.P. site has continued to receive attention by those researchers who study Great Lakes prehistory. However, this "attention" has been confined primarily to professional circles and associated publications. Consequently, other than through my own public lectures here in the Upper Peninsula, the general population of this entire region has received little information about this important early Michigan prehistoric site.

Of course, a detailed account of how John Gorto and I came to find this remarkable cache of Late Paleo-Indian relics has never been published. I hope to change all of that by authoring this narrative that draws its information not only from the various Deer Lake project work sheets and documents recorded during our archaeological survey, excavation, and site material analysis, but--for the first time--I have disclosed in my own written words the story of the actual discovery of the site as recorded in my personal field notes that were hand scribbled into my field book back at the time of that landmark find.

But certainly, this story would not be complete if it were left merely to words contained in a penned narrative. It's been said many times that a single picture is worth a thousand words. As an historian and an archaeologist, I fully understand the power of that truism. As such, I am also going to tell the story of the

Gorto Site discovery by sharing in this book my private collection of never-before published photos, most of which were taken by my father Bob Paquette and I to document this historic project. They are the priceless documentation photos that seized forever, in precious solitary frames of captured time, some of the most exciting moments I ever experienced during my ongoing quest to uncover evidence of our Lake Superior region's first pioneers. Let each single picture contained in this book write its own thousand words in the annals of our region's history.

Although in my mind it seems like it happened only yesterday, the footprints that John Gorto and I left behind in the mud along the shoreline of Deer Lake on that fateful day have long since faded away into the past. Indeed, those very footprints have now joined those of a once forgotten band of Paleo-Indian hunters who so very, very long ago walked those same steps on that very shore.

I know now that what John and I discovered lying amidst the sand and the rocks on that eroded shoreline ridge overlooking Deer Lake was indeed the find of a thousand lifetimes. It was a landmark discovery of the necessary archaeological evidence that was needed to prove to the living world that the People had blazed their first trails into the heartland of the Upper Peninsula of Michigan near the end of the last Ice Age.

But at the same time, John and I had discovered something far beyond a treasured archaeological collection of rare 10,000-year-old Paleo-Indian artifacts. For from those cold stone ancient spear points, there emanates a faint voice that whispers to each of us a timeless message from the far distant past, proclaiming to everyone the eternal truth that our roots of humankind run very deep into this sacred land that is beneath our feet.

James Robert Paquette

Let the journey into the far distant past begin....

****

Figure 1: Jim Paquette (left) and John Gorto shaking hands on the morning of March 22, 1987 at the exact spot of their historic archaeological discovery on Marquette County's Deer Lake.

Chapter 1

It was a day of sadness for the small band of Paleo-Indians who had made the long precarious trek into the North Country to hunt the elusive caribou near the shores of the Great Freshwater Sea. They stood huddled together upon the crest of a windswept ridge overlooking a small inland lake that from this day forward would forever be sacred in the hearts and minds of the People. Death had come to Neemaibee, one of the male members of their small group, and now, they joined together to bid final farewell to the spirit and body of their loved one.

The women and children had spent the day gathering a huge pile of dried jack pine branches and spruce boughs from the surrounding forest, while the men had busied themselves building a wooden platform upon which they laid Neemaibee's body. To prepare their fallen kinsman for his eternal journey, they dressed him in a fine caribou skin parka and then armed him with an incredible array of hunting spears, all tipped with magnificently crafted stone points. Other things, now lost in time and forever unbeknownst to us, were also placed alongside his body.

After the gathered wood was carefully heaped about the crematory platform, all was ready. The People gathered together and watched as a fire was kindled near the base of the huge brush pile. Within minutes, the crescendo of crackling snaps from the burning pine merged with human cries and lamentations to form a sorrowful dirge that shattered the omnipresent silence of the primeval boreal forest. As the People sorrowfully gazed into the inferno, they could feel the skin on their weathered faces tighten in response to the scorching heat that poured forth from the crematory fire. One by one they stepped back away from the intense heat, never taking their tear-filled eyes off of the hallowed flames that consumed the earthly remains of their fellow clansman Neemaibee. In time, the flames subsided and the doleful task was finished. The People--and time--moved on.

Somewhere in the neighborhood of ten thousand winters have come and gone since that proposed drama was played out by real-life Paleo-Indians who once lived--and perhaps died--near the shores of Deer Lake in Michigan's Marquette County. For it was there, on March 21, 1987, that avocational archaeologists John Gorto and I literally stepped upon one of the most remarkable prehistoric sites ever found in the Upper Great Lakes region. That site is known today as the Gorto Site (20MQ39). Located just twelve miles inland from Lake Superior near the northern outskirts of the historic mining community of Ishpeming, the Gorto Site provided the first irrefutable evidence of Early Man's past existence in Michigan's Upper Peninsula. A treasured cache of no less than thirty-four individual whole or fragmented Late Paleo/Early Archaic period projectile points was uncovered in situ during our 1987 archaeological excavation project at the site.

Figure 1A: Gorto Site Cache/Great Lakes Cody Scottsbluff Projectile Points
A. Hixton silicified sandstone (Hixton); B. Hixton; C. Hixton; D. Hixton; E. Hixton; F. Hixton.

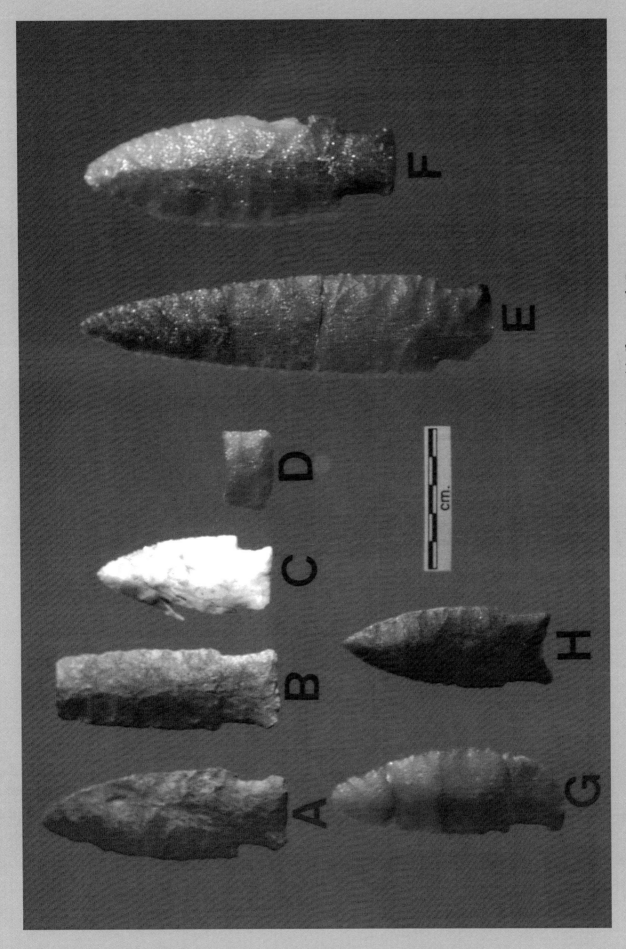

Figure 1B: Gorto Site Cache/Great Lakes Cody Scottsbluff Projectile Points
A. Siltstone; B. Siltstone; C. Quartz; D. Hixton; E. Hixton; F. Hixton; G. Hixton; H. Hixton.

Figure 1C: Gorto Site Cache/Great Lakes Cody Eden Projectile Points
A. Hixton; B. Hixton.

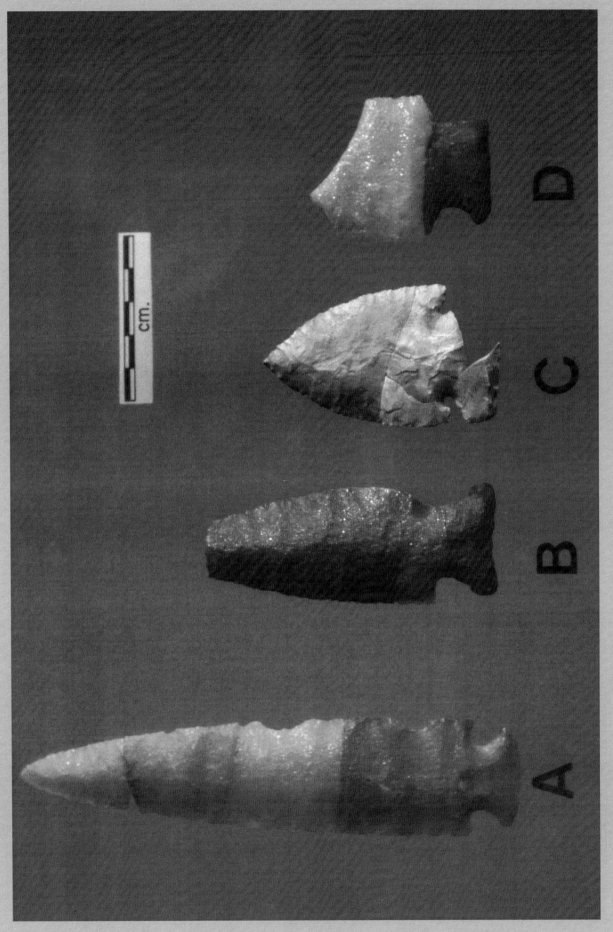

Figure 1D: Gorto Site Cache/Early Archaic Side-notched Projectile Points
A. Hixton; B. Hixton; C. Chert; D. Hixton.

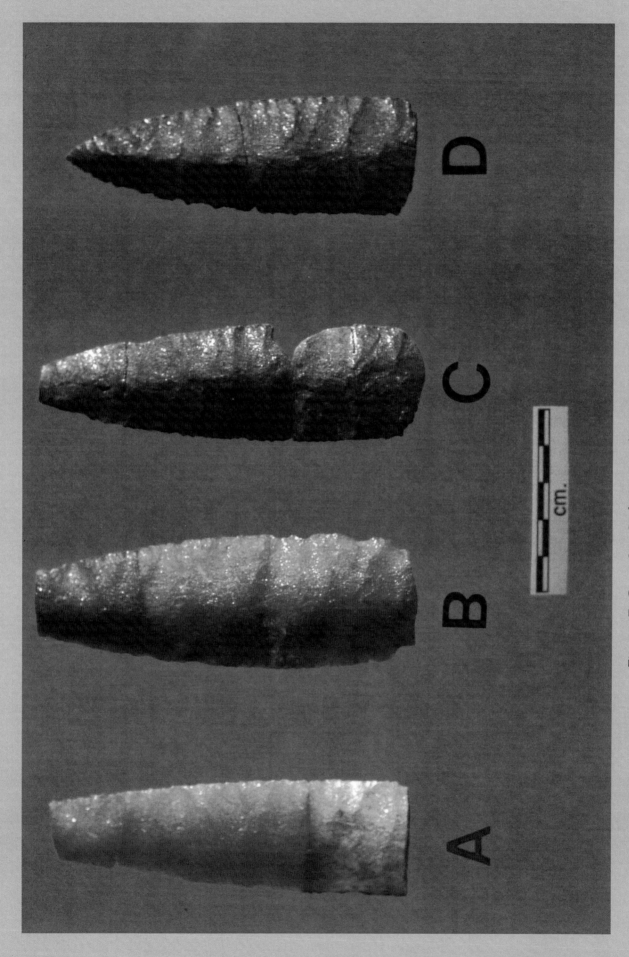

Figure 1E: Gorto Site Cache/Projectile Point Blade Fragments
A. Hixton; B. Hixton; C. Hixton; D. Hixton.

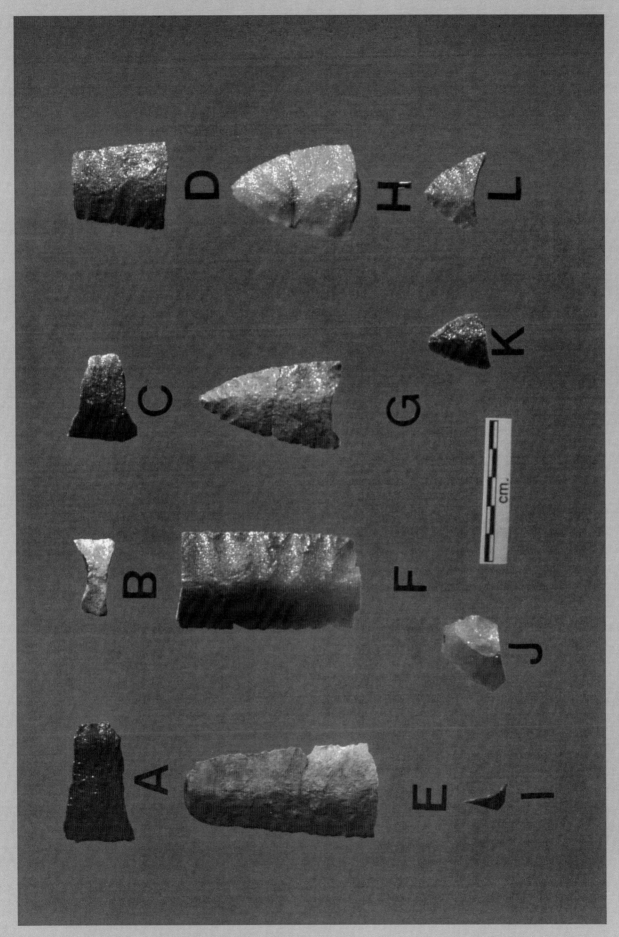

Figure 1F: Gorto Site Cache/Miscellaneous Projectile Point Fragments
A.- D. Hixton; E. Siltstone; F.- L. Hixton.

For me, the discovery of this incredible collection of ancient points marked a true milestone in my ongoing search for the truth about our past. Intensive research, thoughtful interpretation of existing archaeological data, plus a heavy dose of good ol'Yooper common sense had convinced me that the footprints of my own Native American ancestors were once mingled amidst the tracks of the Ice Age fauna that roamed the melting fringes of the dying Greatlakean ice sheet as it grudgingly receded northward across the Upper Peninsula. And like all past human cultures, I knew that these ancient peoples would inherently have left behind some form of physical evidence to mark their brief passage through life on this planet. A broken spear point per chance, the half-buried remains of an ancient hearth, a simple stone scraper--somewhere out there, like a beacon shining forth from the distant past, was the hard evidence that would surely shed the light of knowledge upon our meager understanding of the coming of the People upon this land. Perhaps on the eroded shoreline of an ancient inland lake, maybe in the powdery dust of some timeworn footpath, it would be there.

On an otherwise uneventful spring morning back on May 12 of 1984, I committed myself to the arduous task of piecing together the ancient puzzle of Marquette County's prehistoric past. It was on that day that I set out upon the quest to find that missing archaeological evidence. Back at that time, virtually nothing was known about any of the early prehistoric cultures and peoples who had surely once inhabited the vast interior upland regions of the Central Upper Peninsula. In fact, previous to my research and field study, no one had ever documented even a single Paleo-Indian artifact discovery anywhere in the entire U.P. For me, it was indeed going to be that proverbial search for a "very small needle in a VERY big haystack."

Amazingly, my initial search for that elusive physical evidence met with near instant results as on the very first day that I began my archaeological survey, I located a buried cache of ancient copper artifacts as I walked along the northern shoreline of Teal Lake. In the days that followed, I intensified my search along the forested lakeshore for additional artifacts and soon discovered a series of ancient campsites in this very same area. Incredibly, all of these prehistoric sites were located just mere minutes away from the front steps of my house.

Figure 1G: It was in this exact location on the north shore of Marquette County's Teal Lake that I first discovered the long lost archaeological key that would unlock the doors of scientific inquiry into this area's unknown prehistoric past. The discovery of ancient Native American copper and quartzite relics on May 12, 1984 within the city limits of my hometown of Negaunee set in motion my ongoing search for evidence of the first People who once lived in the Upper Peninsula of Michigan.

Figure 1H: My daughter Jill Paquette holds in her hands a large copper "pikc" that was one of the many ancient copper artifacts that I recovered from the Negaunee Site on Teal Lake during the spring and summer of 1984.

This unexpected discovery of ancient copper and quartzite artifacts within the city limits of Negaunee shattered many preconceived notions about the origins of man in this area, as researchers suspected that the ages of these Teal Lake sites were several thousand years older than any other previously documented site in the Upper Peninsula. The assemblage of native copper artifacts strongly suggested that Archaic Period Old Copper Culture peoples had once lived on the lake, perhaps some three to five thousand years ago. But what was even more exciting was the discovery on Teal Lake of an assortment of ancient stone tools—most of them fashioned from local Agibik quartzite—that lead researchers to speculate that the Teal Lake sites could possibly date back some 8000 or more years! For me, it really was a dream come true. The doors of scientific inquiry into this area's past were thrown open as archaeologists and prehistorians from throughout the region took notice of this new discovery and began to ponder its implications.

Figure 1I: The report of my unexpected discovery of ancient copper and quartzite artifacts on Teal Lake in Negaunee caused the professional archaeological community to take immediate notice. In the summer of 1985, the Negaunee Historical Society and Northern Michigan University co-sponsored an archaeological survey and excavation project at the Teal Lake sites. This project produced additional important evidence that lead local archaeologists to openly suggest, for the very first time, that ancient bands of Native Americans had once lived in the central Marquette County area *at least* 8000 years ago.

In retrospect, I know now that the true value of this initial discovery was not in the questions that it answered, but in the questions that it asked. To be sure, the chance uncovering of such an early prehistoric site right in my own hometown served only to heap more fuel on the fire that burned in my heart. But of the hundred of questions that sprang forth in my mind at that time, one more than any other took hold of my spirit and energies: When did the very first humans set foot into the Upper Peninsula of Michigan? At what exact point in eternity did Grandfather and Grandmother of the People blaze their opening trail into this land and, for the very first time, gaze upon its pristine vistas?

Stirred by a burning desire in my heart to find the answer, I intensified my search in the areas surrounding Negaunee, and in the latter days of summer in 1985, I once again hit the archaeological jackpot with the discovery of yet another ancient campsite on the shoreline of nearby Goose Lake. This very large prehistoric site--known today as the Paquette Site--produced an incredible array of very early stone tools along with thousands of quartzite flakes that were left behind by the ancient toolmakers who had once lived near this inland lake. Based on typological similarities to Paleo-Indian age tools found elsewhere in the western Great Lakes region, archaeologists who studied the Goose Lake artifacts surmised that these stone knives, scrapers and other associated tools "*probably*" belonged to some of the very earliest peoples who once lived in the Upper Peninsula of Michigan.

Figure 1J: It was the incredible assemblage of ancient quartzite artifacts that were recovered from the Teal Lake Negaunee Site and from the nearby Goose Lake Paquette Site that caused researchers, including myself, to speculate that these sites were perhaps Late Paleo-Indian in age. Examples of such artifacts are pictured here, including a large quartzite biface and several Hixton silicified sandstone flakes that were excavated by the Northern Michigan University crew during the 1985 survey project on Teal Lake.

However, the Negaunee Site (20MQ32) on Teal Lake and the Paquette Site (20MQ34) on nearby Goose Lake only served to tease us with tantalizing hints of their true antiquity. For sure, the cultural material that was recovered from these sites looked to be very, very old. But we just couldn't be absolutely sure **how old** because the artifact assemblages that we discovered in 1984 through the fall of 1986 all failed to provide us with that one all-important tell-tale diagnostic artifact that would, once and for all, convince the archaeological world that these sites dated all the way back to the waning years of the last glacial epoch. More specifically, no distinctive early projectile points that once belonged to this region's Paleo-Indian hunters were uncovered *in situ* during those first early days of my archaeological survey. And without the documented discovery of one or more of these unique ancient stone spear points, we could only guess at the actual age of the sites that we had found scattered about the shorelines of central Marquette County's ancient inland lakes.

But then along came the first day of spring in 1987, and with it came the find of a thousand lifetimes. Just three years into the search, the Holy Grail that I had been seeking to offer as proof to the world that my theories on the early origins of man in this area were indeed correct, took the form of the Gorto Site. I remember well the circumstances surrounding this extraordinary and historic archaeological discovery.

Chapter 2

The series of events that lead to the unearthing of this ancient and priceless treasure actually began a year earlier when the Deer Lake Reservoir in Ishpeming Township had been drained as part of a remedial action program that was designed to help clean up mercury contamination in the basin. After the water level in the 906-acre impoundment was drawn down during the winter of 1985-86, the original 100-acre Deer Lake was exposed along with the eroded remnants of its former shoreline. John Gorto was the first to walk these ancient hallowed grounds in search of prehistoric sites that same year.

Figure 2A: In the winter of 1985-86, the 906-acre Deer Lake Basin was drawn down to its original 100-acre lake size as part of a remedial action plan by the Michigan Department of Natural Resources and Cleveland-Cliffs Inc. to help clean-up mercury contamination in the reservoir. That following summer, John Gorto was the first to seize this golden opportunity to conduct an archaeological survey along the exposed eroded shoreline areas of the lake and the adjacent river banks of the Carp River inlet and outlet. The "original" lake and its Carp River inlet are shown above in the late summer of 1986.

At John's request, I had also visited the lake several times later that fall to join him in the search for additional sites and surface artifacts. Our initial joint survey efforts on Deer Lake in 1986 produced some very exciting and promising results as we were able to locate and salvage numerous stone artifacts that were found lying fully exposed atop the eroded barren surface of the drained reservoir bed. Just as they had at the Negaunee Teal Lake sites and at the nearby Paquette site on Goose Lake, the ancient stone tools that John and I surface collected from numerous small prehistoric campsites that dotted the area surrounding Deer Lake appeared to be extremely old. However, our early surface survey of the area, once again, failed to turn up that much sought after diagnostic projectile point that would provide the key to unlock the messages contained in the artifact collections that we had acquired thus far.

Figure 2B: Early in the fall of 1986, I joined Gorto (photographed above walking the drained basin bed near its north shoreline) in the search for archaeological sites and artifacts on Deer Lake. We were hoping that sooner or later we would discover that all-important diagnostic projectile point that would prove to the world that Paleo-Indians once lived in the central highlands of the Upper Peninsula of Michigan.

Figure 2C: During our 1986 surface survey of the drained Deer Lake Basin bed, Gorto and I found a wide-range of historic and modern-day artifacts, including numerous boat anchors, lost fishing poles and fishing lures, old bottles and other 19th century "garbage" left behind by the past local residents of the Deer Lake Location, plus the remains of one very old sunken wooden row boat, as seen pictured above.

As the late fall days of 1986 slipped by, our search along the eroded lake shore of Deer Lake only intensified as there was no doubt in our minds that we were getting closer and closer to finding the elusive proof. Surely, an ancient Paleo-Indian stone spear point—that most important missing corner piece of the entire archaeological puzzle—was out there somewhere. We simply had to keep on searching the drained basin bed while remaining focused on the fact that it was only a matter of time before we would finally come across that one sure thing that would erase all doubts about the antiquity of Marquette County's prehistoric sites.

Figure 2D: Besides the many historic artifacts that we found lying exposed upon the drained basin bed, Gorto and I also discovered numerous prehistoric artifacts such as the ones shown here. These early Hixton silicified sandstone and quartzite flake tools strongly suggested that there were Late Paleo-Indian sites on the lake. However, without the discovery of even one diagnostic Paleo-Indian spear point, we could only guess at the age of the artifacts and sites that we had located on Deer Lake in 1986.

However, winter befell us before John and I could systematically and thoroughly survey the entire shoreline area surrounding the small lake. With the coming of the cold and the snow of November, there was simply no choice but to end the search for the time being. And so, like a couple of Lake Superior Country black bears, John and I settled into our hibernation dens to wait it out until spring to continue our hunt. Five long months later, the weeping blanket of wasting snow finally released its icy grip from the surrounding countryside as a rash of record high temperatures struck an early *coup de grace* to Old Man Winter. And with the coming of an early thaw, our relentless search along the eroded shoreline of Deer Lake resumed.

I remember that day like it was just yesterday. It was Saturday, March 21, 1987. It was the first day of spring. The sun was shining brightly in a near cloudless blue sky while a warm spring southern breeze licked up the last of the melting snow bank that sat in front of my house on Clark Street. Certain that enough bare ground would finally be uncovered in the areas surrounding Deer Lake to make a surface search for artifacts worthwhile, I decided that it was time to try to interest my partner John in a trip to the drained basin bed to continue our ongoing archaeological survey.

The idea to call John had initially entered my mind earlier that same day while my wife Karen and I were driving along Highway US 41 on our way back home from a late morning shopping trip to Marquette. Just as we were approaching the Carp River bridge near the eastern outskirts of Negaunee, I plainly remember a very strange thing that happened. I was cruising up the highway, sitting there soaking in that warm spring sun that was radiating through the closed car door window, when all of sudden I started thinking about how absolutely great it would be to finally get back out to Deer Lake when I got home. After all, that sun was shining so very nice, the snow was melting away, and for sure, some of that southern exposed shoreline along the lake would be free from the passing winter's ice and snow cover.

As I was thinking about the lake and envisioning myself being out there, a very strong feeling or a premonition (I'm not sure what to call it) came to me: ***"TODAY is going to be THE day that I am going to make an incredible archaeological find on Deer Lake!"*** When that particular thought hit me, I vividly remember looking over towards Karen and saying these words, "I'm going to go to Deer Lake today and I'm going to find a Scottsbluff spear point."

I actually blurted out those exact words, "I'm going to find a Scottsbluff spear point." Of course, Karen simply turned her head towards me for just a second and gave me a strange look. It was a cross between the "You're getting way too much sun on your head!" look and the "Yah! Right!" look. I knew what she was thinking, and I could understand her reasoning for the "look."

After all, a Scottsbluff spear point, mind you, is a very specific type of a Paleo-Indian projectile point that was used by some of the western Great Lakes region's earliest human inhabitants. Archaeologists refer to these ancient peoples and their cultural components, including their very distinctive Scottsbluff and closely related Eden projectile points, as the "Cody Complex." Based on research that surrounds a handful of radiocarbon 14 dates secured from outside of the Great Lake's area, it is thought that this early projectile point tradition probably existed in portions of North America from approximately 10,800 to 9800 calendar years ago. Now, also keep in mind that not a single person had ever found and documented even **one** of these early definitive stone time-markers anywhere in the Upper Peninsula of Michigan up until the time that I made that surprising Saturday afternoon declaration to Karen. Scottsbluff Paleo-Indian projectile points were indeed "rarer than partridge teeth" here in the U.P.!

But, in any case, those were the **exact** words that I said to my wife. Somehow I had visualized in my mind that I was really going to do it. TODAY—March 21, 1987—was going to be THE DAY that I would make the find of a thousand life times! Call it a premonition, call it ESP, or you can call it just an incredible lucky guess. But, I actually thought it, and then I said it out loud.

Anyway, shortly after we arrived back home in Negaunee, I dialed that fateful phone call to John Gorto.

John's immediate answer was an enthusiastic, "Yes! Let's get going!" He further added that it was a strange coincidence that I had called him as he was sitting at home just getting ready to call me for the very same reason. We quickly ended our phone conversation, and less than a half an hour later we were both standing near the shoreline of Deer Lake, eager to re-embark upon our journey into the far distant past.

As we stood there looking across the still ice-covered lake, I thought once again about my "premonition" and about what I had said to Karen. Then, as the two of us stepped forward to begin our search, I remember saying to John, "Well, let's go find us a Scottsbluff spear point!" And with those prophetic words still ringing in our ears, John and I stepped into the mud and set out upon an unforgettable trek into the pages of history itself.

TODAY was indeed going to be THE DAY.

We quickly circled around the frozen, swampy west end of the lake and walked along the north shoreline until we reached a rather large snow-free area at the northeast corner of the lake. It was there, along the gentle slopes of a barren shoreline ridge, that John and I had surface collected a small number of miscellaneous artifacts during our hurried walkover survey the fall before. Knowing that we were definitely on an archaeological site, John and I began a very slow, deliberate examination of the exposed surface area. Scanning the sand and gravel deposits that lay between the many small patches of melting snow was tedious and difficult as singular stone artifacts blended in extremely well with the natural backdrop of rock and mud. Our initial efforts turned up absolutely nothing and caused John to comment at one point, "We can't even find a single flake!"

However, our diligence paid off for just shortly after he had uttered those words, I located a small surface concentration of quartz and quartzite waste flakes that had been left behind by an ancient knapper. A few minutes later, John came across the broken blade section of what appeared to be a large quartzite projectile point. We both inspected the point fragment and concluded that it looked to be very old. However, the telltale base of the point was missing, so we didn't know exactly what type or style of projectile point it was. Thus, we couldn't determine the probable age or cultural affinity of the artifact. Something else that we didn't know at the time was that the point fragment that we had just found was actually from a nearby archaeological treasure trove of very special Paleo-Indian artifacts. It was, in fact, a portion of the very treasure that we were seeking, but due to our inexperience at that time in working with Paleo-Indian lithic artifacts, we simply didn't recognize it as such —YET.

Figure 2E: After sitting out the long U.P. winter, our search for ancient sites on Deer Lake finally resumed on March 21, 1987. Melting snow and ice still obscured much of the surface area around the lake's shoreline. This photo of John and I searching between the snow patches at the northeast corner of the lake was taken the following day shortly after we arrived that morning at the newly named "Gorto Site."

After examining the immediate area for the missing base section but coming up empty-handed, we continued our search along the ridge. We zigzagged back and forth for just a short period of time before John yelled out to me, "Hey Jim! You gotta come see this!" He quickly followed that with the chuckling words, "Well, maybe you don't want to see it."

By the tone of his voice and judging from where he was standing, I could plainly see that John had found something in the exact spot area where the two of us had just previously searched. As I quickly approached John, who was now kneeling over his find, I commented, "I suppose you found something right in one of my tracks."

"No, but darn near, " John answered back. My answer to that was "You gotta be kidding," as I hurried my pace, knowing that John had discovered something very, very special. And then, as I scurried up to his side, he excitedly exclaimed, "You're not going to believe it. Look at this!"

I looked down to where John was pointing, and there, just inches away from the end of his fingertip was an absolutely perfect Scottsbluff Paleo-Indian projectile point laying completely exposed upon the rocky gravel. "Oh my God!" I muttered aloud as I instantly dropped to my knees next to John. With a trembling hand, I slowly reached down and gently touched the edge of the incredibly ancient relic with my fingertips.

Figure 2F: "Hey Jim! You gotta come see this!" With those words still ringing in my ears, I knelt down next to this perfect Late Paleo-Indian Scottsbluff projectile point that lay fully exposed in the gravel. As I reached down to touch it with my finger tips, I remember thinking, "We did it!"

Suddenly, John blurted out, "Here's another one!" as he pointed to a second Scottsbluff point laying just a short distance from the first one. As I continued to stare in utter amazement at the ground beneath us, I noticed yet another point, and then the fragment of another!

"Here's another point!" John cried out.

"And here's one over here!" I quickly followed as my scanning eyes picked out an additional point stem protruding from the gravel.

Figure 2G: "Here's another one!" This absolutely incredible Great Lakes Cody Scottsbluff projectile point lay within inches of the first one that we found.

The ground beneath us was, quite literally, a prehistoric collage of ancient spear points and point fragments. We had stumbled upon the find of a thousand lifetimes--a large *in situ* surface concentration of diagnostic Late Paleo-Indian projectile points. It was a find so rare, a discovery of such significant archaeological value, that it is hard to truly describe the flood of emotions that overwhelmed me at that incredible moment of discovery. Howard Carter had surely not felt any greater sense of personal triumph at that extraordinary instant when he first peered into the long-sealed tomb of Tutankhamen, nor could Don Johanson have experienced a deeper feeling of reverential astonishment as he reached out to brush away those first grains of sand from the fossilized bones of Lucy.

Figure 2H: "And here's another one over here!" We were in disbelief. The ground beneath us seemed to be covered with ancient spear points (this photo is of three Hixton Scottsbluff points lying together in the gravel). It was, in the truest sense, the find of a thousand lifetimes!

As we knelt there in a numbed state of euphoria over our great fortune, I suddenly remembered what I had said earlier in the day to my wife while on our ride back from Marquette, and then again, what I had said to John when we first got to the lake. It gave me mental goose bumps as I wondered what it was that could possibly have tipped me off to the fact that this incredible moment was actually going to happen TODAY. To this very day, so many years later, I still wonder—and I still smile to myself every time I think about it.

Anyway, at that point, John and I began to talk in earnest about, "Okay, what do we do now?" Astutely aware of the magnitude of our find, we realized immediately that we had to leave all of the artifacts undisturbed so that the site could be documented and properly excavated by a professional archaeologist. Then, and only then, would any and all possible doubts be erased about the early origins of man in the Upper Peninsula of Michigan. Surely, the critical information and new data that would be recovered as a result of a professional excavation of an undisturbed Paleo-Indian site would be worth far more than the artifacts themselves if they were simply picked-up only to be showcased in either John's or my own personal collection. The treasure we had sought and found, after all, did not belong to us; it belonged to the ages and to all mankind, to human generations past, present, and future.

After a very short conversation on the issue, John and I both agreed to leave the points undisturbed and to contact the proper people immediately about our discovery. Mind you, I have had to do some tough things in my life, but try to imagine what it was like to simply walk away and leave behind a true treasure trove of 10,000 year old Paleo-Indian projectile points sitting high and dry in an exposed area where there was certainly the possibility that anyone else could come along and find them before we could return. It was indeed a very hard thing to do, but it was also the **right** thing to do. And so, after taking one long, last look at that incredible surface concentration of Scottsbluff/Cody Paleo-Indian spear points, we finally took leave of the site in order to make the necessary contacts.

Figure 21: John and I had found a treasure beyond our wildest dreams—a large *in situ* concentration of diagnostic Late Paleo-Indian projectile points (shown here is yet another Great Lakes Cody Scottsbluff point). But we knew that it was not ours for the taking. For the true treasure to be gained lay within the information and the knowledge that would be gathered if the site was left perfectly intact by John and I so that it could be studied and excavated by a professional archaeologist.

When we arrived back at John's house a short time later, the very first thing that we did was to call Northern Michigan University archaeologist Dr. Marla Buckmaster. Marla wasn't home at the time, so we left a rather excited message on her answering machine proclaiming that John and I had just discovered a Late Paleo-Indian site on Deer Lake. We told her to call John immediately upon getting the message. It was certainly a phone call unlike any that Marla had ever received in the past--a message that would soon change her life forever.

I'll admit that the very next thing that John and I did after hanging up the phone was to each grab a celebratory can of cold beer from John's fridge. Certainly, the very finest of expensive champagnes wouldn't have tasted any better that day than that first very special gulp of cheap beer! As we sat there clinking together those aluminum beer cans in a triumphant toast, I thought for the first time about what name we should give to the site when registering it and documenting its location with the State of Michigan's archaeologist's office. It didn't take me more than a few seconds to decide--on my own-- what the site would be called.

I would insist on naming the site in John Gorto's honor as he was the very first person to recognize the research potential of the drained basin bed, he was the very first person to search the shorelines of Deer Lake in 1986, he was the very first person to touch one of those incredible Scottsbluff spear points earlier that day, and he was the person who invited me along, and ultimately, allowed Jim Paquette to share in this greatest of archaeological discoveries. And thus, I made the decision sitting right there at John's kitchen table that this very special site would forever be known as the "Gorto Site."

Shortly after I shared my personal thoughts with John on the name that I would give to the site, I left for home where I tried unsuccessfully to contact Michigan's state archaeologist Dr. John Halsey at his office down in Lansing. But after all, it was a late Saturday afternoon. I did however get in touch with another Upper Peninsula professional archaeologist, John Franzen, who lived in the Escanaba area and worked for the U.S. Forest Service. To say the least, John was very excited about our discovery. He said that he would try to join us on our project to help out in any way that he could as soon as he could free up from other commitments.

Later that evening, Marla finally caught up with that "frantic" phone message from John and I on her answering machine. She immediately returned the call. To say that there was pure excitement in the air would be putting it mildly. In any case, quick plans were made over the phone to visit the "Gorto Site" the following day.

Figure 2J: In lasting recognition of John Gorto's contributions to Upper Peninsula archaeology, I had decided on the day of our discovery of that incredible cache of ancient spear points on Deer Lake that the site on which they were found would forever be known as the Gorto Site. John is pictured above working the screen box at the Gorto Site on March 23, 1987 with Deer Lake in the background.

Chapter 3

Bright and early the very next morning we were back on Deer Lake. John and I arrived at the site first, along with my father and noted local photographer, Bob Paquette, who had joined our small team of volunteers in order to photographically document this historic discovery and the day's events. As soon as we arrived on the site, we quickly relocated the surface concentration of Scottsbluff points and immediately set about the task of shooting the initial documentation photographs of that treasured collection of ancient Upper Peninsula artifacts.

As my father set up his equipment and meticulously prepared for a close-up shot of that first *"Hey Jim! You gotta come see this!"* Scottsbluff point that John had discovered the day before, I paused to savor the moment by simply watching my Dad go through his motions. And as he snapped the shutter and took the picture of that timeless human artifact, I smiled in my heart, for it seemed that I was somehow in a wonderful dream that was way too good to be true. After all, I remember thinking, what could possibly be better than this? John and I had shared the discovery of a thousand lifetimes the day before, and now my own father was sharing in what was going to be one of the most significant archaeological projects ever undertaken in the Upper Great Lakes region. It was plain to see very early on that it was going to be another great day!

Figure 3A: To help us photographically document our historic March 21 discovery, we returned to the site the following morning with noted award winning photographer Bob Paquette from Negaunee. He's also my Dad. I took this great photo of my father as he was setting up to shoot the very first photo of the *in situ* Paleo-Indian projectile points.

Figure 3B: This was the first photo that I took on the morning of March 22 shortly after we arrived at the site. It's a photo of Gorto Site "artifact #1." It's the very Scottsbluff projectile point that John had <u>first</u> pointed to on the previous day. I still couldn't believe it, but there it was after some 10,000 winters—the elusive hard evidence that I had been seeking to prove to the world that shortly after the end of the last Ice Age, WE WERE HERE.

We had just completed our initial phase of photographing the *in situ* surface artifacts when we finally caught sight of a trio of fellow time travelers off in the distance. It was Marla Buckmaster, archaeologist John Anderton from Negaunee, and John's wife Lois, making their way towards our location along the still frozen southern shoreline of the lake with their shoulder packs filled with equipment from NMU's archaeology lab. Upon arriving at the site after their 3/4-mile hike, Buckmaster, Anderton, and Lois finally got their first look at the incredible collection of Paleo-Indian projectile points laying on the surface. At that point, I am sure that they also felt that they had joined me in the same dream that this moment in time **was** "way too good to be true."

Thinking back to that moment, I guess I would have to admit that it really **was** a dream of sorts--for it was a dream come true for each and every one of us who was there that morning.

Energized by the discovery and eager to begin the excavation of Michigan's first documented Scottsbluff/ Cody Late Paleo-Indian site, we wasted no time in getting started. Marla took charge of the project as we flagged off the immediate area surrounding the surface concentration with bright orange surveyors' tape. Then, we systematically re-located and photographed each projectile point and point fragment in its exact position on the ground. All of the ancient stone artifacts were clustered together in an area no larger than an ordinary dining room tabletop.

Figure 3C: Shortly after arriving at the site, Dr. Marla Buckmaster from Northern Michigan University (far left) taped off the area of the surface concentration of Late Paleo-Indian projectile points with the aid of NMU archaeologist John Anderton (far right) while my father Bob Paquette (center) readies his camera. I took this photograph looking to the S-SW across the drained basin bed. The far SE corner of the original Deer Lake (still ice-covered) can be seen in the photo behind Anderton.

Figure 3D: After flagging off the surface concentration of projectile points with surveyors' tape, we set about trying to locate every single surface artifact that lay within the taped off area. John Anderton is shown carefully searching the ground for additional artifacts.

Figure 3E: Dr. Buckmaster sets up the directional arrow to point due north in preparation for shooting the documentation photographs of one of the surface artifacts that is directly in front of the letter board. Every surface Late Paleo-Indian projectile point and/or point fragment that was located at the site was photographed in the exact position that it was found.

We then very carefully searched the adjoining areas for additional artifacts. Incredibly, lying just a few scant yards to the south, we located a second but much smaller surface concentration of Paleo-Indian projectile point fragments. We were able to ascertain, at that time, that the large blade fragment that John had picked up the day before had been associated with this second surface concentration.

Figure 3F: With the archaeologist's trowel pointing directly at the artifact, the set-up for the documentation photograph of Gorto Site projectile point #1 is complete.

Figure 3G: Another example of a documentation photograph taken of one of the Gorto Site projectile points. This complete Great Lakes Cody Scottsbluff point was designated as artifact #2 in our field notes and on the square sheets. It is made from a fine-grained siltstone and is one of the few points in the assemblage that was not crafted from Hixton silicified sandstone.

When all of surface artifacts were finally photographed, Buckmaster directed the laying out of two adjacent 2m x 2m excavation units directly over the largest of the two surface concentrations. With these critical control limits in position, we then measured and recorded on our site documentation square sheets the precise locations of all of the surface artifacts located within the stringed boundaries of the twin excavation units.

Only after each artifact was carefully photographed, and then meticulously plotted, were we finally able to pick up the ice cold, stone spear points and cradle them in the warm palms of our hands.

Figure 3H: With the necessary photographic documentation of the surface artifacts completed, Dr. Buckmaster supervises the layout of two adjacent 2m x 2m test units directly over the concentration of Late Paleo-Indian projectile points. Lois Gorto (kneeling center) holds the tape measure for John Anderton while John Gorto looks on. This photo was taken looking to the west at the still ice-covered Deer Lake in the background.

Figure 3I: John Gorto holds the end of the tape as we plot the exact location of each and every surface artifact found in the two test units. The measurements were recorded and the artifacts' precise positions within the units were then meticulously drawn in on the excavation unit square sheets.

Figure 3J: Only after each and every artifact was photographed and then carefully plotted on the test unit square sheet were we finally able to pick up those remarkable Late Paleo-Indian projectile points and hold them in our hands. Here, Marla smiles as she gets the honor of picking up Gorto Site artifact #2--a perfect Scottsbluff point.

To be the first human being in some ten thousand years to embrace a Paleolithic entity of such superb craftsmanship was, for me, a true spiritual experience that allowed my inner soul to break free from those restricting bonds of time that shackle the existence of our consciousness to the present. As I clutched those aged stone treasures in my hands, my spirit was released from those confining boundaries that define and mark this present moment in time. I felt something inside of my being free itself as my spirit ventured back into the ageless mists of the eternal past. And for one precious, timeless moment, I felt the warm living human touch of the transcendental persona of the Ancient One who had once sculptured from stone these magnificent objects that embodied the very essence of his past existence as a nomadic Paleo-Indian hunter. I had, in fact, been touched by the very soul of Grandfather of the People.

One did not have to be committed to spiritualism on that incredible March day back in 1987 to have sensed that we were not alone as we stood huddled together upon the crest of that windswept ridge overlooking Deer Lake.

Figure 3K: My father Bob Paquette shot this timeless photo just as I picked up Gorto Site artifact #1 and cradled it in the palm of my hand. To be the first human being in some 10,000 years to take hold of this precious artifact was for me a true spiritual experience that transcended time. I felt in my heart a kindred bond with the ancient Paleo-Indian hunter who had last clasped this incredible spear point in his own hand so many, many lifetimes ago.

Figure 3L: John Gorto picks up and then holds in his hand Gorto Site artifact #14—an astonishing example of Late Paleo-Indian workmanship. Crafted from a beautiful orange-brown colored piece of Hixton silicified sandstone, this extraordinary Scottsbluff point was the last of the complete unbroken projectile points to be found during our excavation project. Interestingly, all the rest of the points recovered from the two test units were "mysteriously" broken. Eventually, our job would be to figure out "why?"

Finally, our work that day was completed and it was time for us to leave. The first phase of the excavation project was itself now history. After making certain one last time that all of the precious artifacts were properly put away, we packed up all of our equipment. Then, one by one, we marched off to the west in the direction of the sinking late afternoon sun. With our priceless treasure of surface artifacts carefully tucked away in our field bags, we walked silently in single file along the frozen southern shoreline of Deer Lake. Reluctantly, we all returned home from our trip into the past.

It had indeed been a great day to be alive!

Chapter 4

Early the following morning we were back at Deer Lake. Our team was joined by archaeologist John Franzen, who had agreed to contribute his particular skills to the project by plotting the exact location of the test pits with his surveying equipment. While John busied himself shooting the coordinates of the site, we began the actual excavation of the two adjacent test pits. To be totally honest, although we had hopes, we had no great expectations that we would uncover any additional artifacts buried under the surface concentration. We were already "happy campers" and coming up empty handed from the subsurface testing would actually have been "OK" with any one of us at the time as we were perfectly satisfied with the incredible surface artifacts that we had previously recovered from the site the day before.

Figure 4A: It's the beginning of Day 2 of the excavation project! Gorto and Buckmaster (pictured above) started excavating in the west test pit #1 while John Anderton and I tackled the east test pit #2. We had no great expectations whatsoever that we would find much of anything when we began the slow process of peeling away the soil cover with our sharpened trowels. We were in for an unexpected but very pleasant surprise.

But as we began to peel away the layers of sand and time, it soon became evident that the surface artifacts had been merely the tip of a Paleo-Indian iceberg. There were more artifacts--**many** more. Only now, there were no perfect undamaged spear points to be found. Instead, a large concentration of broken projectile points surfaced from beneath our excavating tools. The shattered artifacts were so plentiful and densely clustered that we quickly resorted to excavating with paint brushes so as not to move and disturb them prior to the necessary photographing and plotting.

At first, the damaged condition of the points had us miffed. Why were they so broken up? Why weren't we finding any additional perfect, undamaged projectile points?

As we more carefully examined the fragments as they surfaced, a likely explanation of why the points were in such a shattered condition soon became obvious to us. More and more of the artifact pieces were discolored, or blackened—or **burned**. That was it! The projectile points had once been subjected to a source of very intense heat and we were now uncovering their fire-fractured remains.

However, the answer to the big question "How and why were they burned?" would have to wait until the completion of the excavation itself. For now, our goal was simply to methodically uncover, document, and collect the physical evidence that lie buried at the site. Of course, we all knew that this physical evidence, as it continued to surface in the test pits in the form of fire-fractured stone artifacts, was certain to initially present the excavation team with many more questions than answers. Hopefully, the answers would come to us later on when we would finally get the opportunity to study and to research the evidence.

And so, onward we brushed.

Incredibly, our daylong excavation of that first 5 cm level produced an additional 43 artifacts, all of them being ancient projectile point fragments!

Figure 4B: As soon as we began to scratch the surface within the two excavation units, we hit pay dirt. Numerous pieces of fractured projectile points began to appear in level #1 of both units, including blade fragments of all sizes, shattered tips, and broken bases. It was immediately evident that the incredible surface finds we had documented and collected the day before had been merely the tip of a Paleo-Indian iceberg.

Figure 4C: Because the point fragments that we were uncovering in level #1 were so numerous and densely concentrated, we quickly resorted to excavating the units with paintbrushes so as not to disturb and move the artifacts. In a true literal sense, we found ourselves "brushing away the sands of time" that had long covered this ancient Upper Peninsula treasure trove.

Figure 4D: Another photo of the dense concentration of fractured projectile points that we uncovered during our excavation of the first 5 cm level. Based on the blackened, fire-damaged appearance of many of the Hixton point fragments, such as those pictured here, we quickly ascertained that the points had once been subjected to very intense heat. The obvious fire-fractured condition of the Gorto Site stone spear points would be a major clue that would eventually help us unravel the mystery of what "probably" happened at this exact spot so many thousands of years ago.

Figure 4E: Pictured above is Gorto Site artifact #44 as it lay in test pit #2. It was yet another amazing unexpected find—the base, shoulder, and partial blade section of an early side-notched projectile point. It was one of four Early Archaic side-notched points that we found during the excavation of the Gorto Site cache. The discovery of these diagnostic Early Archaic period artifacts in direct association with diagnostic Late Paleo-Indian Plano artifacts offered researchers important evidence related to early cultural interactions. At the same time, this incredible mixed assemblage of projectile points may, in fact, serve as direct evidence of a Late Paleo-Indian culture in transition.

Figure 4F: Although we were extremely careful not to mistakenly "toss out" any artifacts that we were uncovering during our excavation of the two test pits, there was always that slim chance that we were going to miss something. That's where the value of the screen box comes in. I am pictured above as I very carefully sift through the sand and gravel that I have just taken from test pit #2 to ensure that we don't discard even the tiniest bit of physical evidence. Archaeologist John Franzen can be seen in the background shooting in the all-important location coordinates of the site and the test pits with his surveyor's equipment.

Figure 4G: Critical archaeological evidence can come in many forms, including simple soil differences within the excavation units. In this photo, Anderton and Buckmaster carefully document potential clues in the floor of test pit #1 as they measure and then draw in the differing soil compositions and colorations on the excavation unit square sheet.

Figure 4H: As we uncovered the many projectile point fragments during the excavation, we marked their specific positions with the small flag-topped metal stakes that are shown in the photograph. This made it much easier to see the locations of each individual artifact when taking the documentation photos (such as this one) of the excavated levels within the units. This photo of the completed level #1 illustrates the fact that the vast majority of the artifacts were concentrated in a relatively small area near the juncture of the adjoining test pits.

Figure 4I: Day #2 of the Gorto Site excavation project had been as a complete success and it was time to pack things up. Buckmaster, Gorto, Anderton and Franzen stop to talk about and reflect upon a day on Deer Lake they will all remember for the rest of their lives. Right after I took this photo of the crew standing near the excavation units in the late afternoon sun, I joined them. It had indeed been a great day to be alive!

For sure, Day 2 of the Gorto Site excavation project had been another rousing success as we had set up the test units directly over the remains of an ancient Paleo-Indian feature that was filled with artifacts. Once again, we had hit archaeological pay dirt!

However, all good things must come to an end, and in the immediate days that followed, it became nearly impossible for the members of the small volunteer project team to coordinate our time together to continue working and excavating on the site. And even though the calendar said it was spring in the UP, in reality, it was really still late winter here in Lake Superior Country. Mother Nature soon reminded us all of that when a major April "spring" snow storm dumped 24 inches of "winter" on the shoreline of Deer Lake.

But what was especially troubling for us was the fact that the Deer Lake dam (located on the Carp River outlet) had been ordered closed. Thus, the clock was now ticking as the spring run-off waters flooded into the basin. Without the assistance of a professional archaeologist to continue the work at the site, John and I found ourselves in the frustrating position whereby we could only sit and wait as the rising water levels in basin crept ever closer and closer to the test units. Those were very trying times for John and I, to say the least, as we were very aware of the fact that the clock was indeed ticking, and the precious time that we had left to complete the Gorto Site project was quickly going to run out. And, "run out" it did.

Chapter 5

In the end, we were only able to work at the site on just three more occasions before the rising waters in the reservoir finally filled our excavation units on May 20. A sixty day window of unbelievable "once in a thousand lifetimes" opportunity had come--and was now gone. The good news was that an additional 22 projectile point fragments were recovered from the two test pits during those three (April 10, May 3, and May 5) later visits to the site.

Figure 5A: The date is May 5. The dam had been ordered closed and as can be seen in the photo, the rising water in the basin is now within a few yards of the test units. In just a matter of days, water would once again cover the site area.

Figure 5B: This is it--our very last day of excavating at the Gorto Site. I am shown here on May 5 cleaning up level #4 in the west half of test pit #2. The pit walls show obvious signs of weathering from the many days they have been exposed to the elements. Even at this deeper level, the Gorto Site continued to give up its secrets as I uncovered yet another large Hixton blade mid-section and what we believe was a post mold. The projectile point mid-section was labeled as artifact #116. It was to be the very last artifact that we would recover from the Gorto Site cache.

Also, our May 3 and May 5 excavations at the site uncovered the probable remains of two post molds that were positioned directly within the Gorto Site feature. This surprise discovery offered us dramatic evidence that an ancient structure of some sort had probably once been built right on this very site. These two post molds would later offer us another important clue as to what may have happened on this spot so many, many years ago.

Figure 5C: On my final day excavating at the site on May 5, I noticed this conspicuous round dark stain in the soil as I cleaned the floor of level #4 in test pit #2. We thought that it might be a post mold—the shadowy partial remains of a Paleo-Indian structure of some sort. We had good reason to suspect that this soil stain was exactly that, for just two days earlier on May 3, Buckmaster had uncovered a very similar stain in test pit #1 that she determined was a post mold after cross-sectioning and profiling it. Likewise, we cross-sectioned the above photographed soil stain. It turned out to be a twin to the suspected post mold found in test pit #1 as both exhibited alike parallel sides that clearly terminated in a point.

More good news was that on a follow-up visit to the site area, John recovered the entire missing base portion of that very first broken projectile point that we had discovered back on March 21. When the newly found fractured base section was fitted together with the large blade fragment that John had found earlier, it turned out to be a beautiful Scottsbluff projectile point. It was yet another piece of incredible Paleo-Indian treasure!

But the bad news was that we did not get to complete the excavation of either of the two test units, nor did we get to test any of the areas directly adjacent to the excavation pits. Likewise, we were unable to expand our test excavations to include the nearby second surface concentration of Paleo-Indian points. Most certainly, more artifacts and additional valuable archaeological evidence lay buried within the immediate areas of the excavation site.

For the rest of my life, I will always wonder what it was that we left behind at the Gorto Site back in the spring of 1987. What unanswered questions about the coming of the People into Lake Superior Country could we have answered if our team had been able to take better advantage of the short time that we had been afforded to dig for such clues from the past? On the other hand, I do take solace in knowing that whatever it is that we failed to uncover is still there, sitting under ten to twelve feet of protective Deer Lake water. Someday, who knows. Maybe we'll get back out there to see what treasured relics--and answers--were left behind.

Figure 5D: I snapped this photo of a forlorn looking John Gorto standing in the rain near the water-filled test pits on May 22, 1987. The Gorto Site excavation project was now officially over. A sixty day window of unbelievable "once in a thousand lifetimes" opportunity to investigate an intact Upper Great Lakes Late Paleo-Indian/Early Archaic archaeological site had come---and was now gone. What treasures did we leave behind? What answers still lie buried at the site?

But speaking of "treasured relics," the **really** great news was that when all was said and done, we were able to salvage an incredible assemblage of 89 early projectile points and/or point fragments from the Gorto Site during our excavation project. The vast majority of the points exhibited very distinctive Paleo-Indian traits such fine collateral to horizontal transverse flaking, lanceolate blade shape, and heavy lateral edge grinding of the base hafting elements.

Again, only a precious few of these ancient artifacts were intact, as most of what we recovered were broken pieces of projectile points. In a true sense, it was as if we had found an ancient stone jigsaw puzzle that some 10,000 years ago had been jumbled up and tossed on to the ground. Of course, once we got all of the recovered artifacts up to Northern Michigan University's archaeology lab in Marquette, our immediate job at hand was the chore of fitting all of these stone jigsaw puzzle pieces back together again. And thus, with a couple of bottles of Elmer's Glue and big ol'bucket of patience, we started the slow, tedious task of matching together the dozens and dozens of projectile point fragments that lay in front of us on the lab table.

It took many, many hours of "does this go here this way or does it go there that way?" But due mainly to a Herculean effort by John Anderton and Marla, all of the collected pieces were finally matched and organized. Once again, the results were absolutely astounding!

Figure 5E: Absolutely astonishing artifacts. There isn't much more that I can say about these remaining photographs of some of the incredible projectile points from the Gorto Site cache. The photos themselves say it all, for they are indeed worth a thousand words each that will forever help tell the tale of what happened to John Gorto and Jim Paquette on that first day of spring back in 1987.

Figure 5F: Another priceless ancient treasure from the Deer Lake Gorto Site cache!

It was possible for us to identify fifteen Plano/Great Lakes Cody projectile points and four Early Archaic side-notched points. The firm stylistic similarities between the Gorto Site points and nearly identical specimens from sites that were radiocarbon dated in other areas of North America clearly indicated that the Deer Lake area was once visited by early Holocene hunter/gatherers who had lived during the Late Paleo-Indian/Early Archaic period (ca. 9500 to 8800 RCYBP or 10,800 to 9800 Calendar Years BP).

Figure 5G: A good close look at two more of the Gorto Site projectile points.

They were the Children of the Ice Age that I had sought!

In addition to these 19 identified points, at least 15 and possibly as many as 18 other early projectile points were represented by various other fragments. Except for five of the points, all of the artifacts were manufactured from a gem-like stone known as Hixton silicified sandstone—a fine-grained pseudo-quartzite that was a much preferred raw material among the very earliest cultures of people who once lived throughout the western portions of the Great Lakes Region. The source of this highly distinctive stone is from a single large deposit known today as Silver Mound located in Jackson County, Wisconsin near the small town of Hixton. Incredibly, this primary source of Hixton silicified sandstone, or "sugar stone" as it is sometimes called due to its characteristic sparkling appearance, is over 350 kilometers as the crow flies—that's over 215 miles cross country—from the Deer Lake Basin!

Interestingly, nearly all of the fragments exhibited obvious evidence of having been fractured by exposure to intense heat. In other words, they appeared to have been intentionally burned. This revelation certainly begged the question: Why would these ancient Peoples have burned and ultimately destroyed what certainly must have been among their most valued possessions? For sure, their very lives as far-ranging nomadic hunter/gatherers were dependant upon these precious projectile points. What compelling reason would have led them to do such a thing?

Our subsequent research pointed us towards a likely explanation as a thorough study of the literature revealed documentation of other past discoveries in the Great Lakes Region of similar caches of heat-fractured Paleo-Indian artifacts that were very much like the Gorto Site collection. Two of these sites, Renier and Pope, are located a relatively short distance to the south of the Upper Peninsula in east central Wisconsin. At these two particular sites, numerous fire-damaged Scottsbluff/Eden and Cody-Eared points were recovered that were stylistically very similar to the Cody projectile points found at Gorto. The Renier site also produced several other types of heat-fractured artifacts, including fragments from a single Early Archaic side-notched point. This, again, paralleled the Gorto Site where four Early Archaic side-notched points were also found directly associated with numerous Late Paleo-Indian Scottsbluff/Eden points.

But besides the stone relics, the Door County Renier Site excavation produced something else that was very special--something that ultimately unraveled the mystery to the site investigators Ron and Carol Mason of what they had uncovered. Found scattered amidst the fire-fractured stone artifacts were numerous fragments of burned calcined human bone. It was clear evidence that left little doubt that the archaeologists had excavated the remains of an ancient Late Paleo-Indian cremation burial.

Figure 5H: This is as fine a Paleo-Indian artifact as one could ever hope to hold in one's own hands. Made from the gem-like sparkling stone Hixton silicified sandstone, this remarkable conjoined Great Lakes Cody Scottsbluff projectile point from the Gorto Site exhibits obvious tell-tale signs of having gone through an intense fire at some point in time in the far distant past. All in all, the Gorto Site cache certainly was "the find of a thousand lifetimes!"

Likewise, the Pope Site collection of heat fractured projectile points that was later found in nearby Waupaca County was similarly interpreted as being the remains of a ceremonial cache of burial goods associated with a Late Paleo-Indian Great Lakes Cody cremation.

Although we had found no bone fragments nor any definitive evidence of human internment on Deer Lake, comparisons of the Gorto Site feature material with reported data from previously discovered probable Paleo-Indian cremation sites in the Upper Great Lakes region such as the Renier and the Pope sites favored an interpretation that this incredible collection of heat-altered points represented a cache of burial goods associated with a Late Paleo-Indian cremation. We further surmised that the two post molds that we had uncovered in the excavation units back in early May of 1987 may have been the shadowy remains of a crematory platform of some sort. Thus, we concluded that we had probably uncovered the ancient remains of a Late Paleo-Indian cremation burial at the Gorto Site.

In the end, the Gorto Site proved to the world that sometime shortly after the end of the last Ice Age, a small band of Paleo-Indians had indeed made the long precarious trek to the North Country to hunt near the shores of the Great Freshwater Sea. It is our belief that at some point in their journey, they had stood huddled together upon the crest of a windswept ridge overlooking a small inland lake to bid final farewell to the spirit and the body of a loved one. In doing so, they unknowingly left behind the fragile archaeological evidence that marked their brief passage through life on this planet.

Such incredibly ancient human artifacts certainly answered some of our questions about the origins of man in the Lake Superior region. However, by their very nature, archaeological answers always have a way of asking additional archaeological questions, and as I watched the rising waters of the Deer Lake Reservoir inundate the Gorto Site test pits late that spring back in 1987, I for one could not help but wonder who it was who had blazed those first trails into this land that the Scottsbluff/Cody people had surely followed. After all, if the People were already here living in the central highlands of the Upper Peninsula some ten thousand years ago, then maybe they were here eleven thousand years ago, or perhaps even twelve thousand years ago. And if they WERE here eleven or twelve thousand years ago, then somewhere, out there, was something very, very special that they had surely left behind.

My dream--my goal--was to find it. And find it, I did.

But that's another story, for another day.

The End...
...but only of this single leg of our long Journey

About the Author

James Robert Paquette is a native son of the Upper Peninsula of Michigan and a 1974 Magna Cum Laude graduate of Northern Michigan University. Often times described as a "true modern-day Renaissance man," Paquette's passions are many. He is a successful freelance outdoor writer and photographer, an award winning labor journalist and editor, and the author of numerous published articles on relic and treasure hunting.

He is an honored regional historian who has authored many news reports and historical articles for various local and regional media publications. Paquette is also a much sought after public speaker, and has provided frequent lectures and educational programs at universities, local schools, historical societies, and many other organizations.

His greatest passion, however, is prehistoric archaeology. A self-taught avocational archaeologist, Paquette has worked on numerous professional archaeological site surveys and excavations, including the historic 1986-87 Deer Lake Gorto Site project. Recognized as one of the preeminent authorities on Late Paleo-Indian adaptations in the region, he has co-authored and published three major research reports on Great Lakes Late Paleo-Indian archaeology.

Since 1984, Paquette has been conducting a "personal" ongoing archaeological field survey in the central U.P. for the purpose of locating, documenting, and preserving prehistoric Native American sites and artifacts. In the process of uncovering dozens of ancient sites in the rugged highlands of Marquette County, Paquette has documented the earliest archaeological evidence of human occupation in Michigan's Lake Superior country. This treasured evidence provided Paquette with the necessary data that enabled him to prove that ancient Paleo-Indian peoples lived and hunted deep in the heart of the Upper Peninsula near the end of last Ice Age, perhaps some 12,000 years ago.